ASTERIX AND THE CAULDRON

TEXT BY GOSCINNY

DRAWINGS BY UDERZO

TRANSLATED BY ANTHEA BELL AND DEREK HOCKRIDGE

HODDER AND STOUGHTON
LONDON SYDNEY AUCKLAND TORONTO

Australia	Hodder & Stoughton Children's Books, Mill Road, Dunton Green, Sevenoaks, Kent, TN13 2YJ, England
Austria	Delta Verlag, Postfach 1215, 7 Stuttgart 1, R.F.A.
Belgium	Dargaud Benelux, 3 rue Kindermans, 1050 Brussels
Brazil	Cedibra, rua Filomena Nunes 162, Rio de Janeiro
Canada	Dargaud Canada Ltee, 307 Benjamin Hudon, St. Laurent, Montreal, PQ H4 N1J1
Denmark	Gutenberghus Bladene, Vognmagergade 11, 1148 Copenhagen K
Finland	Sanoma Osakeyhtio, Ludviginkatu 2-10,00130 Helsinki 12
France	Dargaud Editeur, 12 rue Blaise-Pascal, P.O. Box 155, 92201 Neuilly Sur Seine
	(*Breton*) Armor Diffusion, 59 rue Duhamel, 35100 Rennes
	(*Langue d'Oc*) Societe Toulousaine Du Livre, Avenue de Larrieu, 31094 Toulouse
German Federal Republic	Delta Verlag, Postfach 1215, 7 Stuggart 1, R.F.A.
Greece	Anglo Hellenic Agency, 5 Koumpari Street, Athens 138
Holland	Dargaud Benelux, 3 rue Kindermans, 1050 Brussels
Hong Kong	Hodder & Stoughton Children's Books, Mill Road, Dunton Green, Sevenoaks, Kent, TN13 2YJ, England
Iceland	Fjolvi Hf, Njorvasund 15a, Reykjavik
Indonesia	Yayasan Aspirasi Pemuda, Jalan Kebon Kacang, Raya 1, Flat 3, Tingkat 111, Jakarta
Italy	Arnoldo Mondadori Editore, Via Bianca de Savoia 20 20122, Milan
Latin America	Ediciones Junior S.A., 386 Aragon, Barcelona 9, Spain
New Zealand	Hodder & Stoughton Children's Books, Mill Road, Dunton Green, Sevenoaks, Kent, TN13 2YJ, England
Norway	A/S Hjemmet (Gutenberghus Group) Kristian den 4 des Gate 13, Oslo 1
Portugal	Meriberica, rua d. Filipa de Vilherna 4-5*, Lisbon
Roman Empire	(*Latin*) Delta Verlag, Postfach 1215, 7 Stuttgart 1, R.F.A.
South Africa	(*English*) Hodder & Stoughton Children's Books,
	Mill Road, Dunton Green, Sevenoaks, Kent, TN13 2YJ, England
Spain	Ediciones Junior S.A. 386 Aragon, Barcelona 9
Sweden	Hemmets Journal Forlag (Gutenberghus Group) Fack 200 22 Malmo
Switzerland	Interpress S.A., En Budron, B, 1052 Le Mont/Lausanne
Turkey	Kervan Kitabcilik, Serefendi Sokagi 31, Cagaloglu-Istanbul
Wales	(*Welsh*) Gwasg Y Dref Wen, 28 Church Road, Yr Eglwys Newydd, Cardiff
Yugoslavia	Nip Forum Vojvode Misica 1-3, 2100 Novi Sad

British Library Cataloguing in Publication Data
Goscinny
    Asterix and the Cauldron.
    I. Title   II. Uderzo   III. Bell, Anthea
    IV. Hockridge, Derek
    741.5'944   NC1499

    ISBN 0–340–20212–2
    ISBN 0–340–22711–7   Pbk

The year is 50 BC. Gaul is entirely occupied by the Romans. Well, not entirely… One small village of indomitable Gauls still holds out against the invaders. And life is not easy for the Roman legionaries who garrison the fortified camps of Totorum, Aquarium, Laudanum and Compendium…

a few of the Gauls

Asterix, the hero of these adventures. A shrewd, cunning little warrior; all perilous missions are immediately entrusted to him. Asterix gets his superhuman strength from the magic potion brewed by the druid Getafix…

Obelix, Asterix's inseparable friend. A menhir delivery-man by trade; addicted to wild boar. Obelix is always ready to drop everything and go off on a new adventure with Asterix — so long as there's wild boar to eat, and plenty of fighting.

Getafix, the venerable village druid. Gathers mistletoe and brews magic potions. His speciality is the potion which gives the drinker superhuman strength. But Getafix also has other recipes up his sleeve…

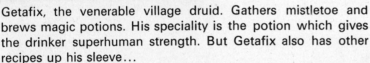

Cacofonix, the bard. Opinion is divided as to his musical gifts. Cacofonix thinks he's a genius. Everyone else thinks he's unspeakable. But so long as he doesn't speak, let alone sing, everybody likes him…

Finally, Vitalstatistix, the chief of the tribe. Majestic, brave and hot-tempered, the old warrior is respected by his men and feared by his enemies. Vitalstatistix himself has only one fear; he is afraid the sky may fall on his head tomorrow. But as he always says, 'Tomorrow never comes.'

THE SPRINGTIME CALM OF THE LITTLE VILLAGE WE KNOW SO WELL IS INTERRUPTED BY THE ANNOUNCEMENT OF AN OFFICIAL VISIT...

IF YOU THINK I'D TAKE A PART IN ANY GLEE WITH YOU, FULLIAUTOMATIX...

ANY MORE SINGING AND YOU GET TAKEN APART! WITH GLEE!

CHIEF WHOSEMORALSARELASTIX AND HIS MEN ARE ON THEIR WAY!

STRAIGHT AWAY A COUNCIL MEETING IS CALLED.

WHO IS THIS CHIEF WHOSEMORALSARELASTIX?

HE'S THE CHIEF OF A VILLAGE ON THE CLIFF TOPS. I DON'T LIKE HIM MUCH; HE'S TIGHT-FISTED AND HE'LL DO ANY SORT OF DEAL WITH THE ROMANS FOR MONEY...

HOWEVER, HE IS A GAULISH CHIEF! WHEN ONE GAULISH CHIEF MEETS ANOTHER GAULISH CHIEF, PROTOCOL MUST BE OBSERVED! LET PREPARATIONS BE MADE TO WELCOME HIM!

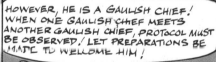

SOON AFTERWARDS...

NOW THEN, BOYS! DECORUM, DIGNITY, NOBILITY!

HERE HE COMES, CHIEF!

WOTCHER, MATE! BIT WARM, EH? HOW ABOUT A JAR?

?!?!...

HAVE YOU COME ALL BY YOURSELF LIKE THAT?

OH, NO! HERE'S MY RETINUE.

?

WHAT THE... IT'S A CAULDRON!

YES, THAT'S WHY I HAD TO WALK. THERE'S NOT MUCH ROOM ON THESE SHIELDS.

YOU MEAN YOU GAVE UP YOUR SHIELD TO THIS CAULDRON? WHAT'S SO SPECIAL ABOUT IT?

IT'S FULL OF SESTERTII, BY TOUTATIS! COME OVER HERE.... I'VE GOT SOMETHING TO TELL YOU.

2A

JULIUS CAESAR IS IN GRAVE FINANCIAL DIFFICULTIES. HE'S USED THE TAXES WHICH WERE GOING TO PAY HIS GARRISONS HERE IN GAUL TO EQUIP HIS ARMIES FOR NEW CAMPAIGNS...

I HEARD THAT CAESAR WAS ABOUT TO LEVY NEW TAXES, SO I PUT ALL MY PEOPLE'S SAVINGS IN THIS CAULDRON, AND I'VE BROUGHT IT TO YOU FOR SAFE KEEPING.... I BELIEVE YOU DON'T PAY ANY TAXES?...

WELL, A TAX COLLECTOR DID SHOW UP ONE DAY... WE HAVEN'T PAID ANY TAXES SINCE!

DEAR ME!... I'LL NEVER FORGET HOW WE SHOWED HIM UP!

WHAT FUN WE HAD! REMEMBER WHEN...?

OH, DO STOP! HOHOHO!

YOU MEAN HE NEVER RETURNED?

THAT'S RIGHT. NO RETURN, NO TAX RETURN NO TAXES!

2B

6

WHEN I KNEW WHAT THE ROMANS INTENDED TO DO I DIDN'T HESITATE! I GRABBED THE FIRST AVAILABLE CONTAINER, THREW OUT THE ONION SOUP SIMMERING INSIDE IT, AND FILLED IT WITH ALL MY SESTERTII..

AND I HAVE BROUGHT IT TO YOU FOR SAFE KEEPING! THE ROMANS WILL NEVER DARE TO LOOK FOR IT HERE!

BUT COULDN'T YOU HAVE HIDDEN THE MONEY... BURIED IT?

NO. THE ROMANS ARE ALWAYS EXCAVATING.... THERE ARE SO MANY BURIED TAXES ABOUT THEY'LL PROBABLY BE GETTING DUG UP FOR CENTURIES TO COME!

IT'S A GOOD IDEA TO PREVENT THE ROMANS GETTING THEIR HANDS ON THIS MONEY....

IT IS, ISN'T IT?

..BUT I THOUGHT YOU WERE IN THEIR GOOD TABLETS... ESPECIALLY AS THE ROMANS LIKE PEOPLE WHO PAY THEIR TAXES REGULARLY.

WHAT?

YOU'VE NO RIGHT TO DOUBT MY PATRIOTISM! I MAY DO BUSINESS WITH THE ROMANS...

.... BUT I ALWAYS MAKE THEM PAY TWICE THE PRICE I'D HAVE CHARGED MY GAULISH CUSTOMERS!

THAT'S GOOD!

VERY GOOD!

AND DO YOU DO MUCH BUSINESS WITH GAULS?

NO.... THE ROMANS BUY EVERYTHING I'VE GOT TO SELL!

VERY WELL, WE'LL LOOK AFTER YOUR CAULDRON UNTIL THE TAX COLLECTOR HAS BEEN.

I WILL PUT IT IN THE HANDS OF MY MOST TRUSTWORTHY WARRIOR: ASTERIX!

8

10

SOON AFTERWARDS...

CHIEF WHOSEMORALSARELASTIX MENTIONED SOME ROMANS... PERHAPS THEY STOLE THE MONEY.

WE'RE NOT FAR FROM COMPENDIUM. LET'S GO AND ASK THEM...

THE ENTRANCE TO THE FORTIFIED ROMAN CAMP OF COMPENDIUM...

HALT! QUO VADIS? NO ENT...

SCHKONNK!

WHERE'S THE INFORMATION BUREAU?

THAT MUST BE THEIR CENTURION'S TENT OVER THERE.

GAULS? WHO GAVE YOU PERMISSION TO ENTER OUR CAMP?

THE CAULDRON.

WHAT CAULDRON?

THIS CAULDRON! WE'VE COME TO FILL IT!

FILL IT? WHAT WITH?

I'M NOT TOO CLEAR MYSELF, BUT ASTERIX CAN EXPLAIN IT ALL.

TO FILL IT WITH MONEY. OUR MONEY! MONEY! DO YOU GET IT? THE MONEY! THE MONEY!

THE MONEY?

THE MONEY!

OUR PAY HAS ARRIVED!

AND NOT A MOMENT TOO SOON!

OUR MONEY! OUR MONEY!

19

ASTERIX, I DON'T REALLY UNDERSTAND BUSINESS. WE HAD FOURTEEN BOARS, WE SOLD THEM, AND...

I KNOW, I KNOW....

I DON'T THINK WE'RE CUT OUT TO BE BUSINESSMEN... THE CAULDRON IS STILL AS EMPTY AS EVER, AND THE MAGIC POTION WON'T HELP US TO...

ENCORE! ENCORE!

?..

BY THE RIGHT... QUICK MARCH!

CLAP! CLAP! CLAP! CLAP! CLAP! CLAP!

ASTERIX, I'VE GOT IT! I'LL TELL YOU WHO'S GOING TO FILL OUR CAULDRON! DOGMATIX!

?!

I'LL TEACH HIM SOME TRICKS, AND PEOPLE WILL THROW US LOTS OF MONEY!

SIGH!

COME ALONG, DOGMATIX! BEG! LIKE THIS!

NOW, ON YOUR FRONT PAWS, LIKE THIS!

ROLL ALONG THE GROUND LIKE TH....

?

WOOF! WOOF! WOOF! WOOF! WOOF WOOF! HARF! HARF! HARF!

19

THE SHOW STARTS...

DING! DONG!

WHAT AN UGLY LOT YOU ARE! WE MAY BE UGLY TOO, BUT YOU'RE WORSE!

YAAAH!

IT'S SO DREADFULLY AUTHENTIC....!

ORGIES! ORGIES! WE WANT ORGIES!

STOP! STOP! THIS IS DISGRACEFUL! THEY'RE MAKING FUN OF US!

HE'S RIGHT!

NO, HE ISN'T! THROW HIM OUT! MUSEUM PIECES! ROMAN RELICS!

THAT'S YOUR CUE! GO ON! GO ON, THEN!

I.... I'LL NEVER MAKE IT!

THINK OF THE CAULDRON!

NEXT DAY, STILL AT CONDATUM, AND...

STILL NOT A SESTERTIUS!

WE COULD SELL THE CAULDRON?

HOW WOULD THAT HELP FILL IT?

I SHALL NEVER, NEVER BE ABLE TO GO HOME TO OUR VILLAGE AGAIN!

THERE, THERE, ASTERIX! I'M SURE TOUTATIS WILL HELP US!

?!?

DONG! DING! TING!

I HATE TO SEE PEOPLE LOOKING SAD WHEN I'M SO HAPPY! I'VE JUST WON A PACKET!

DING! DING! DING!

DING! DING!

?!?!

29A

HEY! WON IT? WON IT HOW?

AT THE RACES, MATE! AT THE RACES!

I ONLY HAD A FEW SESTERTII, I PUT THEM ON A CHARIOT, AND I WON!

WHERE EXACTLY ARE THE RACES?

IN THE HIPPODROME. FOLLOW ME; I'M GOING BACK TO MAKE ANOTHER PILE.

THERE, ASTERIX, WHAT DID I SAY?

THAT'S THE HIPPODROME. WELL, GOODBYE AND GOOD LUCK.

YOU KNOW, WHEN WE DO HAVE A BIT OF CASH FOR ONCE, I HATE TO RISK IT!

BUT THERE'S NO RISK! WE PLACE OUR BET AND WE FILL THE CAULDRON! THAT'S WHAT HE SAID.

29B

35

37

HEY! YOU THERE!

ME?

YES, YOU! YOU LOOK TO ME LIKE SOMEONE WHO'S THINKING OF ROBBING A BANK, BUT YOU HAVEN'T GOT A HOPE!

THE BANK IS CONSTANTLY GUARDED. THE GUARD CHANGES AT NOON, AT SIX IN THE EVENING, AND AT MIDNIGHT, AND THERE ARE MEN INSIDE ALL NIGHT...

THE GOLD IS KEPT IN A CELLAR WITH A HEAVY IRON DOOR WHICH HAS A SECRET CATCH HIDDEN IN THE ORNAMENTAL MOULDING...

TAP! TAP! TAP!

...SO DON'T GO GETTING ANY IDEAS!

SOON AFTERWARDS...

I DIDN'T LEARN ANYTHING. HE SAW THROUGH ME BEFORE I COULD GET ANY IDEAS.

NEVER MIND. WE CAN WATCH THE SENTRIES COMING AND GOING FROM THIS WINDOW.

WE SHALL HAVE TO TAKE TURNS KEEPING WATCH... WRITE EVERYTHING DOWN, INCLUDING THE TIMES...

AND FOR TWO DAYS AND TWO NIGHTS...

... OUR FRIENDS TAKE TURNS.

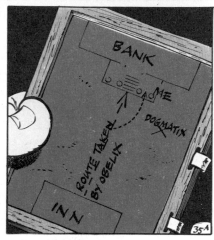

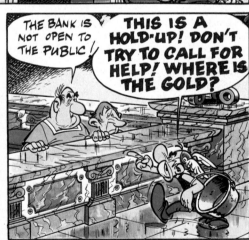

THIS DOOR WILL NEVER STAND UP TO THE MAGIC POTION!!!

BANG!

OH!

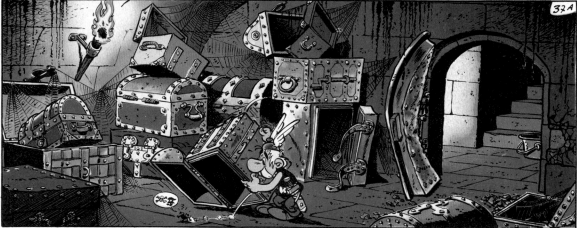

37A

HEY, WHAT ARE YOU DOING HERE? IF YOU WANT TO DEPOSIT MONEY, YOU HAVE TO DO IT AT THE COUNTER UPSTAIRS.

I DIDN'T COME TO DEPOSIT MONEY, I CAME TO TAKE SOME.

BANG!

OH, I THOUGHT IT WAS A BIT STRANGE!

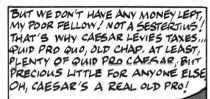

BUT WE DON'T HAVE ANY MONEY LEFT, MY POOR FELLOW! NOT A SESTERTIUS! THAT'S WHY CAESAR LEVIES TAXES... QUID PRO QUO, OLD CHAP, AT LEAST, PLENTY OF QUID PRO CAESAR, BUT PRECIOUS LITTLE FOR ANYONE ELSE. OH, CAESAR'S A REAL OLD PRO!

COME ALONG, OBELIX!

AND STOP THAT WHISTLING!

O.K.

37B

41

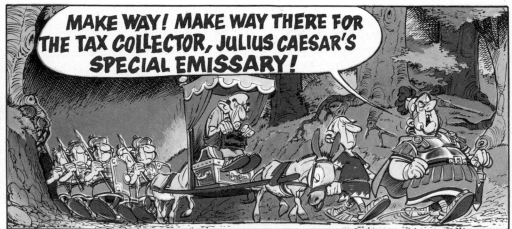

A FEW BRUISES LATER !!!

HAS EVERYONE BEEN DONE?

NOW THEN, HAND OVER YOUR MONEY!

You will be taxed on the sum of which you are about to take possession

I WANT TO FILL MY CAULDRON. IF THERE'S ANY MONEY LEFT OVER YOU CAN HAVE A TAX RETURN.

Your instalment on account will be deductible from the sum finally due.

AWFULLY SORRY... IT'S EXACTLY THE AMOUNT WE NEED... COMING, OBELIX?

A RECEIPT! I WANT A SIGNED RECEIPT!

WE'LL TAKE CHIEF WHOSEMORALSARELASTIX THIS MONEY, AND I SHALL BE ABLE TO GO HOME TO OUR VILLAGE MY HEAD HELD HIGH!

WAIT A MINUTE...?

SNIFF! SNIFF! SNIFF!

SMELL THAT!

BUT MONEY HAS NO SMELL!

SNIFF! SNIFF! SNIFF! SNIFF!

SMELLS GOOD!

EXTREMELY GOOD! COME ON, OBELIX!

THESE SESTERTII SMELL OF ONION SOUP!

YET THEY COME FROM THE ROMAN TAX COLLECTOR'S CHEST!

AND IF THESE SESTERTII SMELL THE SAME AS THOSE YOU ENTRUSTED TO ME, IT'S BECAUSE THEY **ARE THE SAME!**

CLINK!

THAT NIGHT, WHEN YOU CAME TO OUR VILLAGE, YOU TOOK ME ASIDE TO GIVE ME SOME INFORMATION... AND ACTING ON YOUR INSTRUCTIONS, YOUR MEN STOLE THIS MONEY!

YOU USED THE MONEY TO PAY YOUR TAXES, THUS KEEPING IN WITH THE ROMANS, AND KNOWING VERY WELL THAT I SHOULD MOVE MOUNTAINS TO REPAY OUR DEBT!

IN FACT, WE WERE TO PAY YOUR TAXES FOR YOU!

I SEE YOU GET THE IDEA...

43A

YES, I DO GET THE IDEA!

THEN COULD SOMEONE PLEASE EXPLAIN TO ME?

TO ME, MEN!

YOU SEE TO THE REST.

ALL RIGHT, BUT YOU WILL TELL ME AFTERWARDS, WON'T YOU?

WOOF!

I DO HOPE ASTERIX WILL EXPLAIN. I GENERALLY LIKE TO KNOW WHY WE'RE FIGHTING.

42B

PAF!

WOOF! WOOF!